DOWN AT THE BOTTOM
OF THE DEEP DARK SEA

by Rebecca C. Jones • illustrated by Virginia Wright-Frierson

Bradbury Press / New York

Collier Macmillan Canada / Toronto • Maxwell Macmillan International Publishing Group / New York / Oxford / Singapore / Sydney

Bradbury Press, Macmillan Publishing Company, 866 Third Avenue, New York, NY 10022.

Collier Macmillan Canada, Inc., 1200 Eglinton Avenue East, Suite 200, Don Mills, Ontario M3C 3N1.

The text of this book is set in 16 point ITC Korinna Regular. The illustrations are rendered in watercolor. Typography by Julie Quan and Christy Hale.

Printed and bound in Hong Kong by South China Printing Company (1988) Ltd.

FIRST AMERICAN EDITION
10 9 8 7 6 5 4 3 2 1

Library of Congress Cataloging-in-Publication Data
Jones, Rebecca C.   Down at the bottom of the deep dark sea   /   by Rebecca C. Jones : illustrated by Virginia Wright-Frierson. — 1st ed.   p.   cm.   Summary: Andrew hates water and intends to stay away from the ocean while at the beach, but he changes his mind when he needs water for the sand city he is building.
ISBN 0-02-747901-3
[1. Beaches—Fiction.   2. Sandplay—Fiction.]   I. Wright-Frierson, Virginia, ill.   II. Title.   PZ7.J72478Do
1991   [E]—dc20   90-33981   CIP   AC

For Amanda, who emerges triumphant—R.C.J.

To Dargan, Amy, Sarah, Hannah, Georgia, Vincent, Skyler, and Daniel—V.W.–F.

Andrew hated water. All kinds of water.
He hated the water that poured into the tub.
Whenever it started gushing from the spout, Andrew
hid behind the towels and sang a loud song.

Andrew hated the water that ran through the garden hose. Whenever other kids played in the sprinkler, Andrew sat on the front step and tried to stay dry.

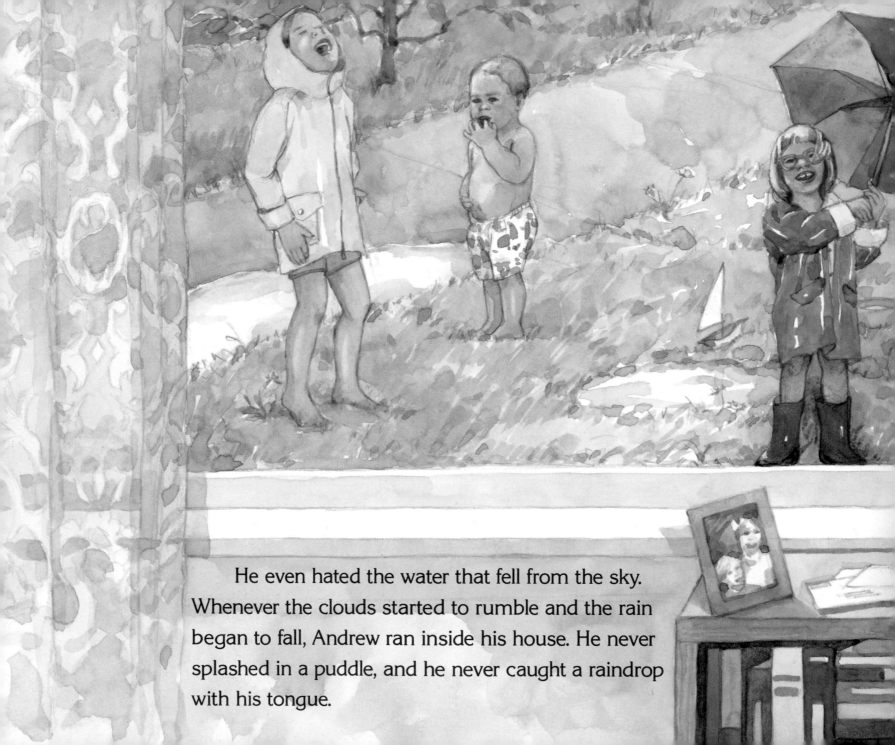

He even hated the water that fell from the sky. Whenever the clouds started to rumble and the rain began to fall, Andrew ran inside his house. He never splashed in a puddle, and he never caught a raindrop with his tongue.

But the worst kind of water was the water at the beach. Far away, it looked deep and dark and very blue.

Up close, it rushed onto the sand with a loud roar that made everyone jump and scream.

Andrew's sister ran into the roaring water. So did his mother and father. They called for Andrew to come in, too.

But Andrew wasn't stupid. He knew what would happen if he went near that roaring water. It would swallow him up, and he would sink—

down to the bottom of the deep dark sea.

And Andrew knew what he would find down at the bottom of the deep dark sea.
Pinching crabs and slimy monsters.

Maybe even a hungry shark or two.

So Andrew stayed away from the water. He started
to build a sand village where it was dry and safe.

He built six little houses, two small gas stations, and
a teeny tiny post office. He put a leaf on a stick and
called it a flag. He stuck the flag on top of the post office.

The post office crumbled.
"I know what's wrong," said a little girl
who was watching Andrew. "Your sand is too dry."

She walked to the edge of the water where the sand
was wet. She filled her bucket with wet sand and brought
it to Andrew. The wet sand stuck together, and Andrew
built a larger post office.

It was the largest sand post office he had ever built.
He stuck a flag in the top, and it stayed fine.

Then Andrew made a school, even larger than the
post office. He built a big department store and an office
building, too.

The little girl kept running to get wet sand, and Andrew kept building.
He was building the largest sand city in the world.

Andrew was just starting to build the world's tallest sand skyscraper when
the little girl's mother said it was time for her to go home.

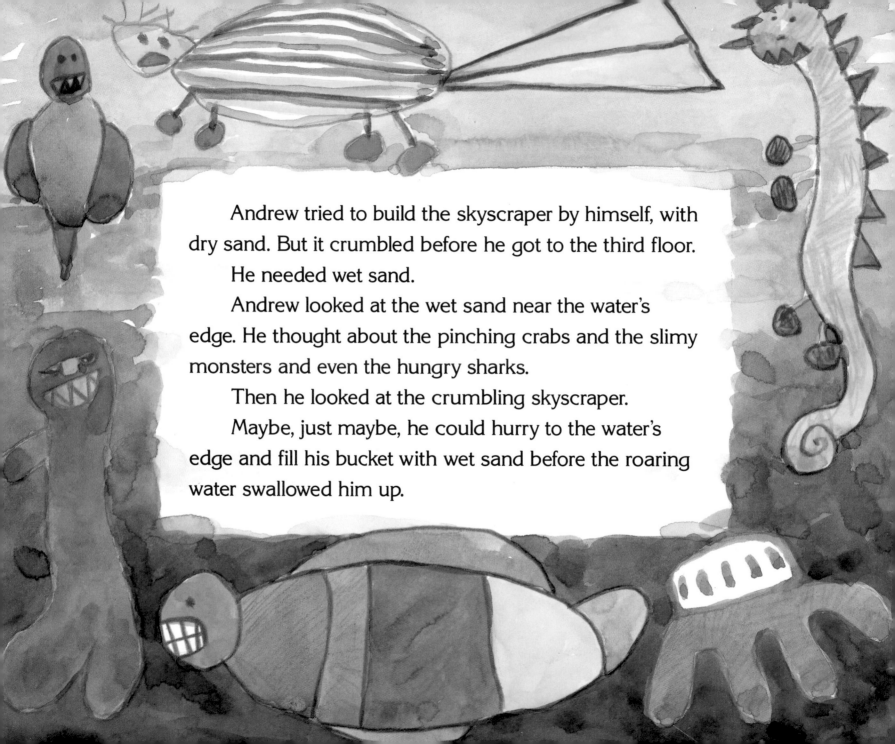

Andrew tried to build the skyscraper by himself, with dry sand. But it crumbled before he got to the third floor.

He needed wet sand.

Andrew looked at the wet sand near the water's edge. He thought about the pinching crabs and the slimy monsters and even the hungry sharks.

Then he looked at the crumbling skyscraper.

Maybe, just maybe, he could hurry to the water's edge and fill his bucket with wet sand before the roaring water swallowed him up.

Andrew tiptoed to the edge of the water and scooped wet sand into his bucket.
Then he ran back to his sand city. The roaring water never even touched him.
Andrew ran back for more wet sand. And more wet sand. And more.

Once the water touched his toes. Once it caught him on the heel. And a couple
of times he fell. But the water never swallowed him up. And he never sank
down to the bottom of the deep dark sea.

Andrew's sand city was getting bigger and bigger
and bigger.

People on the beach stopped to admire the sand
city.

"It's wonderful!" cried a lady with pink sunglasses.

"It's amazing!" cried a man with a hairy chest.

"It's wonderful *and* amazing!" cried Andrew's sister.

"Andrew's all wet!"

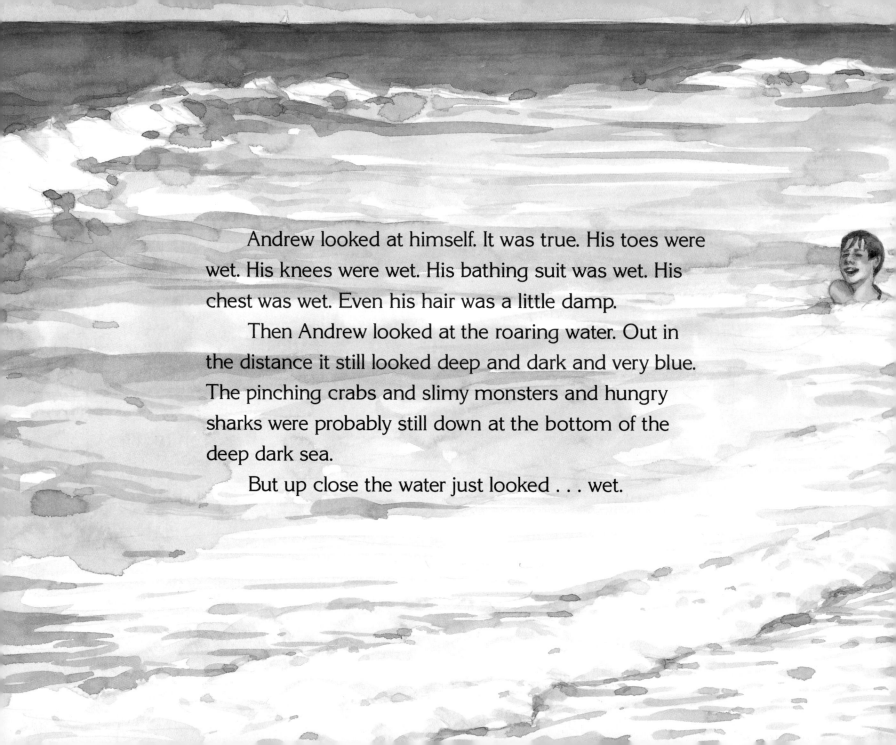

Andrew looked at himself. It was true. His toes were
wet. His knees were wet. His bathing suit was wet. His
chest was wet. Even his hair was a little damp.

Then Andrew looked at the roaring water. Out in
the distance it still looked deep and dark and very blue.
The pinching crabs and slimy monsters and hungry
sharks were probably still down at the bottom of the
deep dark sea.

But up close the water just looked . . . wet.

So Andrew waded into the water and filled his
bucket again.

DATE DUE			

Barcode: 25003339

E   Jones, Rebecca C   94-466
Jon

Down at the bottom
of the deep dark
sea

Church Creek Elementary School
4299 Church Creek Road
Belcamp, MD 21017